Bill Martin Jr, Ph.D., has devoted his life to the education of young children. Bill Martin Books reflect his philosophy: that children's imaginations are opened up through the play of language, the imagery of illustration, and the permanent joy of reading books.

Henry Holt and Company, Inc., *Publishers since 1866*
115 West 18th Street, New York, New York 10011
Henry Holt is a registered trademark of Henry Holt and Company, Inc.
Text copyright © 1996 by W. Nikola-Lisa. Illustrations copyright © 1996 by Dan Yaccarino
All rights reserved. Published in Canada by Fitzhenry & Whiteside Ltd.,
195 Allstate Parkway, Markham, Ontario L3R 4T8.

Library of Congress Cataloging-in-Publication Data
Nikola-Lisa, W.
One hole in the road / W. Nikola-Lisa; illustrations by Dan Yaccarino
"A Bill Martin Book."
Summary: Introduces the numbers one through ten while describing
the people and machinery involved in fixing a hole in the road.
[1. Roads—Maintenance and repair—Fiction. 2. Counting.]
I. Yaccarino, Dan, ill. II. Title.
[E]—dc20 95-41321

ISBN 0-8050-4285-7 / First Edition—1996
The artist used gouache on paper to create the illustrations for this book.
Printed in the United States of America on acid-free paper. ∞
1 3 5 7 9 10 8 6 4 2

To Thelma and her grandchildren
— W. N-L.

W. Nikola-Lisa

One Hole
in the Road

Illustrated by Dan Yaccarino

A Bill Martin Book · Henry Holt and Company · New York

1 One ho

the road,

2 Tw

agmen waving,

3 Three sturd

arricades warning passersby.

4 Fou

oplights flashing,

5 Five

sirens blaring,

6 Six worrie

gineers huddling nearby.

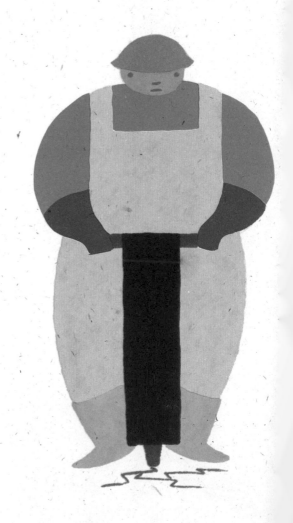

7 Seve

ammers pounding,

8 Eight wat

ipes gushing,

VIDEO

SHOES

ICE CREAM

TOYS

Car

9 Nine storefront

FOOD

COMPUTERS

BOOKS

PETS

looding, *Oh, my!*

10 Ten worker

a flurry,

hurrying, scurrying

ying to fix

One ho

the road.